I'M FOREVER DREAMING

*An Angel Who Fell in
Love with a Demon*

J. SUPERMAD

authorHOUSE®

AuthorHouse™ UK
1663 Liberty Drive
Bloomington, IN 47403 USA
www.authorhouse.co.uk
Phone: 0800.197.4150

Published by AuthorHouse   09/04/2015

ISBN: 978-1-5049-8889-6 (sc)
ISBN: 978-1-5049-8890-2 (e)

Print information available on the last page.

This book is printed on acid-free paper.

CONTENTS

ABOUT THE AUTHOR

Inspired by fantasies, romance, poetry, and fiction over the last few years, this young writer encountered someone who inspired her to the moon and back and has produced a book, its contents holding many secrets.

Choosing to dedicate all pages in the book to one, also encouraging readers to be open to the inspiration hidden in their lives, and finding their unique way to vent and accomplish their ambitions, no matter how far away they seem.

She says that we dream for a reason; ambitions are our motivation, to keep alive, to take another breath, to wake up every day.

"We're all facing the strains of life, whether it's the people, or the place, physical or mental, a helping hand is appreciated more than you think. There may be many times that the things you say either help or hurt, you may not even realize, maybe we need to think before speaking."

"Think about how it would sound in someone's head, be encouraging, I had to climb some steep hills to realize my words meant more than I thought, and this time, I hope they still mean as much."

~ I ~

BEGIN: LET THEM KNOW WHAT IT'S ABOUT

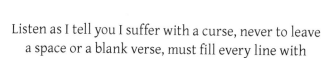

Listen as I tell you I suffer with a curse, never to leave
a space or a blank verse, must fill every line with
a tale to tell, so I'll tell you all about this spell.

It started some time ago now, I met someone
and made a vow, never to sin, never betray,
never to leave in any kind of way.

When people ask what love is, how can they understand,
all I know is I feel unreal everytime you hold my
hand, I'll tell them it's around us no matter what we
do, for me love exists but only when I'm with you.

Each of us hope that we find our soulmate, we
wonder through life gently guided by fate, but
I urge that no one in this world is the same, the
echo in my dreams resemble your name.

They say it's fate that guides us and that someone is there
to find us, but there are a few left at the bottom, they
hold on to the memories, that others have forgotten.

So those forgotten ones need to find a way to stand
out, I write this for them because they need to know
what it's about, they strive to have faith that a door
will open, what lies ahead will forever be unspoken.

Each word I write will reveal the story, the real
one not the one I've let fall before me, see I
hadn't been too trustworthy or too kind at all,
I have to unfold the unaffected original.

I remember in high school I met the girl of my
dreams, she was the most beautiful woman I'd ever
seen, we weren't too young, we shared everything,
but I left her just before we turned eighteen.

I know it was hard for her to see me and then watch me
leave, I bet it didn't help with me asking her to believe,
I kept trying to see her 'till she saw it was true, until
she could tell by my eyes 'I was inlove with you.'

I'm not saying, that her eyes were mistaken, but most
of my thoughts and emotions, I used to fake them, I
can't explain that's just how I was back then, and all
I really needed was what I found in her, a friend.

We became really close, things picked up so fast, and as
quickly as it began, now I'm nothing but her past, that's
what I feared, that I wouldn't be in her life, but why
would she want someone who wants to be her wife.

When the Bible tells us, a woman needs a man, I couldn't
explain my love to them, they wouldn't understand,
I know that you're a woman, but my heart loves
yours, it knows no gender, no race, nothing more.

And this is how I opened my door, in my dreams I see
what I'm searching for, I unknowingly found a way
to stand out, writing is key as I tell you this now.

It started as a way to vent, until an Angel was heaven
sent, those words turned into a display of affection,
I tell her, "Look into my eyes at the reflection."

You've inspired me since I can remember, through every
warm July, every cold November, I kept in inside, but now
I'm ready to show, show them all, everything I know.

You were the girl of my dreams with flowers in
your hair, but the demons in your head made
your world dark with despair, I tried to rearrange
the madness in your mind, so you could take the
love in your soul and leave the rest behind.

A portrait of you could be a work of art, if it captures
your flaws and the storm in your heart, back then it
wasn't easy, we'd both taken strains, but what I'd give
to protect you, through the fire and the flames.

Slowly we unwound the bandage, that hid our lives of
unhealable damage, because with me, you didn't have to
pretend, I loved you more than I could ever love a friend.

&if I could write a book, about how you make me feel,
the title would be something that no one could steal,
"Angels can make all your dreams come true...", when
you hold my hand, I understand the magic that you do.

An enchantment might explain it, I capture and embrace
this, this magic is so blinding unlike I've ever known,
I hold your hand and every fear is overthrown.

When you're here I feel like the best I'll ever be, I love
that feeling you've always given me, it gives me faith, a
reason to believe, that maybe one day we could be free.

I've written this for you if ever you said, that you
had questions about the thoughts in my head, know
I'll wait for you 'till the roses lose red, a door that
begs to be opened, a book that yearns to be read.

I never told you how beautiful you really are, you
shine brighter than the sun, brighter than any
star, nothing compares to your first true love, but
I'm feeling like words can't explain enough.

This is everything I have not said, the thoughts that run
through and through my head, when I look at you I see
the truth, something I never gave to you, so here it is
in black and white, hang onto every word that I write.

Your voice gives me hope among inspiration, love
is a language in no need of translation, if you look
into my eyes I know you'll see, the reflection is what
inspires me, you brought out this side of me, a side
of creativity, someone I wished to always be, it's
only been you, who has made me feel that free.

They say "Don't fall in love, there's just too
much to lose", but my heart &head are at war
and confused, you clear away all the illusions,
make my dreams real, destroying delusions.

I'll write about when we were young, tell them how our
story begun, I helped you up and then broke you down,
swore that I'd changed and promised to stay around.

To those who read it's poetry nothing more, but
for us it's what we've been praying for, for me it's
the words, that I never had the heart to say, the
least I hope is that this brightens your day.

I can remember the sweet sound of your voice,
the way I loved you without having a choice, but
back then I was weak I didn't tell you enough,
that I'd fallen for you, my only true love.

I say when I look back it doesn't feel like me, like
I have two personalities, one's good, the other
is bad, a smart one and one that's just mad.

The first has a tendency to deceive, has the power to
make you believe, believe the webs of lies it creates, as
it draws you in to a morbid place, every word spoken is
just a joke, sets you on fire and laughs at the smoke.

The other one you may prefer, it's world revolves
around only her, endless love, the one who writes,
the one who gives in to all the fights, the one who
loves you too much to leave, it's a shame the other
has to breathe, maybe one day I'll be myself again,
but I still love you in a way that will never end.

Most of my memories they're trying to hide,
I hold them somewhere between regret and
my pride, I say this because I'm not a saint,
a fantasy is what I choose to paint.

I'm always searching, looking to find, find
out about the memories I left behind, I don't
know much but I'll say this because it's true, I
know following my heart leads me to you.

I hope that fate keeps me on your path forever, and
they can always see the two of us together, my heart
pours like the ink with each word written, your
smile keeps me on track &with you I'm smitten.

Me and you are so different but somehow we
connect, without our bad memories things could
be perfect, in my world it's ruled by you, you're
my queen &there's nothing I wouldn't do.

Compared to you no one does it better, so I
write for you this endless letter, so you can
read it once I'm gone, and know that I've been
honest as I dedicate to you, every one.

All I ask is for you to read, it's not a want it's a need,
if you'd chosen not to this book would be a waste,
a waste of the powers you let only me taste, by
the end you'll understand what I mean when I say
this, the only word is magic, I can't explain it.

Life isn't about pleasing everybody,
so just be yourself

~ II ~

HOW WE WERE/THE MEMORIES

I always felt like I was forever falling, falling at your
feet, like every word you spoke, every word made me
weak, daunting thoughts like, is it the idea of love,
I don't know much but I know that it's enough.

Enough to change how I feel inside, to chase
away the demons that hide, and make me
into the person I am, I'll do whatever it takes,
&whatever I can, to let you know that I'm sorry,
but it always comes out wrong, I love the idea
of you and me, and I think that we belong.

I still remember when my life changed, I saw your
face before I knew your name, I'm still not sure if
you were aware, everytime you walked my way, I was
walking on air, I noticed that when you came, you
cleared the sadness and the rain, somehow I lost all
sense of pain, you gave me hope and joy again.

You held my hand close to your heart, trusting me right
from the start, you loved me more than words could
say, some nights you came to me, just to get away.

"They don't know what love is" people would
complain, people that didn't know us beyond our
name, everywhere we went the people were the
same, we thought we only had ourselves to blame.

There were so many problems, there had to be a solution,
you were blinded by my lies, &all the confusion, so
we parted ways, regretting that we'd finished, our
hearts were torn as the love was diminished.

I think about the way things were left, the words
you said after every breath, I think of the plans we'd
sit and make, about our future, we'd stay up late.

I remember when you told me, I love you like no one else
can, I felt so empowered you wouldn't understand, we
should be showing them that nothing can divide us, like
you always said, "There's nothing big enough to hide us."

I try to tell them but they're not listening,
that I pushed you out when you wanted in, no
matter what happened we could never win,
you were the perfect one but I would sin.

It was only me that you opened up to, I don't regret
the things we've been through, I only wish that
I didn't hurt you, the way that I always seem to
do, all you wanted was someone there, but I was
just too young to care, I know I should be where
you are, standing next to you is still too far.

You held my hand through all these years,
chased away the darkness and all of my fears,
you are the one I dedicate this to, never thought
I'd love someone the way I love you.

The time we spent together was much too short; life
was easier when you were my only thought, when I
look into your eyes your powers take over me, feels
like I'm addicted to getting high off of your memory.

I thought I was dreaming when I had you in
my arms, I'd never felt so unreal yet so calm, I
promised myself I'd learn from my mistakes,
as I swept my hand softly across your face.

Our memories are still here, you imprinted my
soul, and I'll continue to write even as I get old,
these words just flow, there's too many to write,
but I give in to it every day and every night.

When we were together I was your rock, your knight,
you were my life support, you made every wrong right,
you'll always have a hold on me that I can never forget,
but I know in your heart that all you feel is regret.

I wounded them all but there was one I believed,
that could destroy the demons that live inside me,
I wondered how she couldn't see, how she could
love someone so easily, to look past all I used to
be, and find what I lost when I chose to leave.

Another night, I greet the moon, now I know you'll
be in my arms soon, you tell me about the times we
shared, I say they've faded from my mind, if you hold
my hand then maybe, they could be there to find.

I know it will take time for me to build up this trust,
I'll do anything to prove that this is much more than
lust, &i know you asked to take things slow, but there
are things on my mind that I need you to know.

Every dream I wish to be true but every fear
keeps me from you, fears like there isn't time
for us to start again, I want you to remember
I have a love that will never end.

All the things I used to say, like how I'd love
you forever &always, I stand by those words to
this day, and every night I'm not with you I will
pray, I'll pray for you to be by my side, I want to
be the best I can be so believe me I'll try.

I have just one question how do I fix this, can I
turn back time turn this hell into bliss, I honestly
don't know what I'd do, if you'd done to me what
I did to you, you know if I could every mistake I'd
undo, you're like a tattoo I can never remove.

I remember one day she made me a band, I remember
each moment as it was pulled over my hand,
nothing expensive but the sentiment was there, I
could see in her eyes deep down she still cared.

The next time I saw her it happened again, my heart
is in love I cannot pretend, I gazed into her eyes
as she placed another band, why these moments
mean the world she may never understand.

The last one she gave me I remember it so clear,
the one that remains I always keep near, as she
handed it to me she said it was for friendship, what
she doesn't realise is, every word I over think it.

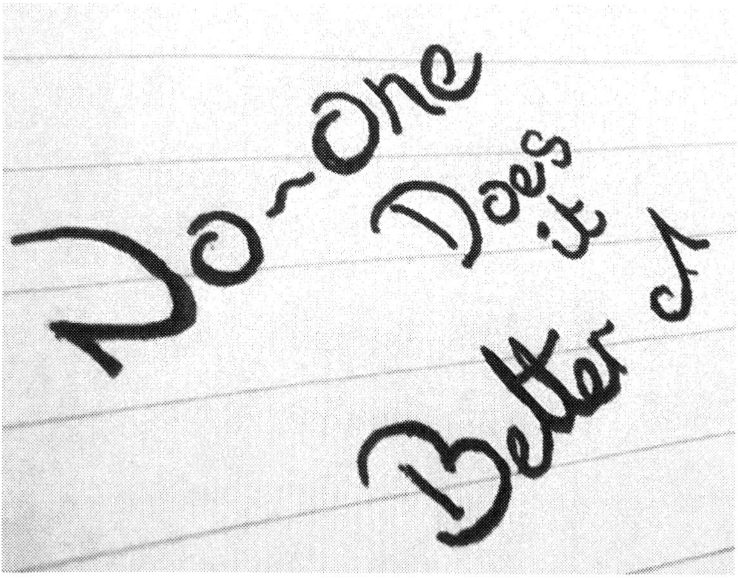
No~One
Does
it
Better

Real feelings dont just go away,
hold on to whatever makes you happy

~ III ~

LET THEM KNOW HOW I FEEL

They say I'm a rhyming inventor so I write it all down,
the thoughts I get when you're not around, but when
you hold me close I wont make a sound, because
when I'm with you my feet don't touch the ground.

I noticed that when I think of you, in my mind it
builds a brick or two, watching as it grows so tall,
something this high makes me feel small, just
wishing I could break down this wall, I tell myself
I can climb it because you'll be worth the fall.

Sometimes I wish that these memories would
leave, I wonder how different things would
be, if someone else had this power held over
me, a haunting curse, for all eternity.

Fairy-tales are just the start, this war between my
head and heart, in my mind I'm thinking logically,
but my heart is not even close to reality.

My imagination feeds off of happiness, it's tasted you
and can't except nothing less, the core supplier to my
inspiration, like I said before, you're God's best creation.

It will take time to replenish your trust, but I
know that this wall seperates us, I'm fading from
your memory, into something worse than an
enemy, something I never wanted to be, I may not
be part of you, but you're still a part of me.

When I left you there was something I found, this is
why I say that to you I am bound, it took a while before I
started to see, there were demons who lived inside me.

With every smile they started to leave, on all my fears
these demons would feed, when you're here you make me
feel strong, you being around keeps these demons gone.

This isn't a puzzle, I don't wish for you to complete me,
I want to be full on my own, I know it wont be easy,
if your love alone, changed me from a liar, maybe the
two of us combined, could set this world on fire.

I know what I feel is love because I've felt it for so long,
you're my definition of perfection, &with you there is
no wrong, I can't put into words what I wish to say, I
just want to make you smile, just to brighten your day.

There's so many things that we have to do,
before I can unveil this book to you, I have
to remind you I'm not who I used to be, and I
thank every reason that you've given me.

But all you ever tried to do was love me and I just left
you to walk away, I'm sat here wishing I could take
back every word I said that day, I crave that feeling you
give me, with you I'm always flying, you tell me to just
be myself because you know how hard I'm trying.

Whenever we talk I always feel defeated, like you know
every weakness, the memory cannot be deleted, I just
get so lost and make things harder than they seem, but
I look back into your eyes and fall deeper than a dream.

I say these days are wasted but never a day that
I write, because I know that these pages will
be held by you one night, I still belong to you
&that's how it will always be, the second our eyes
meet, you know the silence overcomes me.

When I see myself with you I feel that I've changed,
but the demon inside me will always remain, the
part of me that's always saying the wrong thing,
no matter how hard the rest of me is trying.

It's not like I haven't attempted, but I cannot forget
your face, just one thought of you makes my heart
race, a single touch, makes me feel alive, I fall
into a trance as I look into your eyes, I'm aware I
rarely told you what I was thinking, but everytime
you spoke, know that my heart was sinking.

When I get lost I try to look in your eyes, find the answers
to how I feel inside, it could just be us in a place no one
goes, I'll be there for you, tell me things no one knows,
if only things were different, &if only I did not leave,
but I had to walk alone, just to see if I could breathe.

I wish every once in a while I could take you away, we'd
drive until we lose the road &maybe you'd choose to stay,
if you were a charm I'd keep you close to my heart, I'd
wrap a gold chain around you and we'd never be apart.

This will be the first time in a while, you talk to me
and I can't help but smile, feels like forever since I've
been gone, but not a day goes by where I don't hear
our song, the echo plays in the back of my mind,
that's why I hang on to every memory I can find.

When I'm not with you something seems wrong, believe
me I want you not just any one, I want you to learn not
to live without, to find faith amongst all the doubt.

To look through the words that were filled with
rage, to witness the love I've hidden deep in every
page, look past the fact that these are just words, see
that every night I've wished to fly like the birds.

So I've been patient waiting for this to begin,
the day I can let go of what I hold within,
because I've had this desire, a desire to fly, to
be creative, it's what makes me high.

To live for as long as I can survive, to love until my
heart resigns, a desire to love you for as long as
I live, the list is endless to what I would give.

To have you laying by my side, telling me it's been worth
the ride, sometimes I need to talk, wishing that you're
near, saying it was always me is what I want to hear.

I wish I told you everything that was on my mind,
wish we could leave all these bad memories behind,
they just seem to haunt us no matter what we do,
maybe one day we'll be able to break through.

The little things you do, make this wait
worthwhile, and you're the one who sees through
this sinister smile, I want to know your secrets
as I stand beside you, tell me something I don't
know so I can remember something new.

Fate tells me to keep my motives clear, in all my life I've
never been so sincere, I think of the future and what
there is to come, knowing my journey has barely begun.

My heart craves you in every way, I can feel
it pounding as I write this essay, the hold you
have on me keeps me in this maze, and you
know I'll love you until the end of my days.

I hope to always see a path that leads to you, when I'm
lost in the dark, be the light that guides me through,
through my clouded vision you shine brighter than the
sun, brighter than anything, anyone could become.

I cannot control this endless desire, it's not an
obsession, to me you inspire, your eyes leave me
breathless, I think I'm in too deep, I just hope
there is sound whenever I wish to speak.

To hear your voice, for your hand to hold, I'd
trade my last breath, my life and my soul, I
fight because when you're with me it's better,
love is a moment that lasts forever.

Since I left you assumed things have changed, it's
all lies, my heart still feels the same, I've tried
countless times to forget and start over, but this
hold you have on me makes it hard to stay sober.

When I left I knew that nearly ended our story, I thought
we would be stronger and God made you for me, I write
so they know I've lied and to never do the same, never
put someone you love through that kind of pain.

I can't say that you're my number one, that we're like
pickle &cheese, we're older now and leading different
lives, I'm not weak anymore I can't fall to my knees, and
the people who knew us would assume from the start,
that I was the Saint and she'd shattered my heart.

I feel unsettled revealing that this was nothing more
than a lie, through all those years, she'd been the
angel in disguise, beneath her smile she was wounded
inside, but now she's proven that she can be just fine.

I had the strangest feeling that this would set me free,
I don't have the answers but these memories haunt
me, I'll leave our past behind but I won't forget you,
I need to tell them again I write because I have to.

To tell them to love as much as they can with all of their
heart and to go against their brain, because once you've
lost your inspiration, it's something only time can save.

Sometimes I'm indecisive, I never thought it was bad,
until I threw away everything that I'd ever had, I
thought it would bring me closer to all that I'd need,
but being with you was the best place I could be.

Maybe this shows my weakness, I'm hoping that's
not what you see, I want to make it clear, the
faith I have is setting me free, but I'm starting
to feel like my heart's in my mind, maybe once
I've written it all, I can leave it behind.

I can't explain the need to write this down, I
want it to only make you feel proud, you're the
reason for the person I've become, I can live
with my demons but I'd rather have none.

I always say we were young but you know what I
mean, young in our minds like, I wasn't as honest as
I should be, you know all I want is for you read, but I
know right where you are is where you want to be.

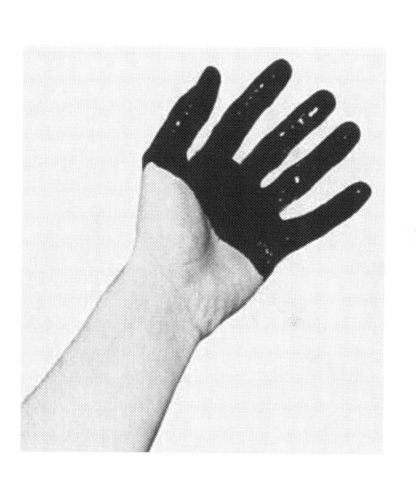

You cant change the past,
so focus on making a great future

~ IV ~

THINKING TO MYSELF

One day you told me you knew I wouldn't leave, my heart is yours, a lifetime guarantee, in paradise I stand, I can only believe it's a dream, when I'm laying next to you, and you're laying here with me.

I've been sitting, thinking of ways to treat you nice, I say you take my hand and my heart flies, though this time you have a disguise, I can't see past all these butterflies.

Past all the fairytale-like curses, that keeps the rhyme flowing in my verses, clouding my vision, you're pure ecstasy, nothing else matters, when it's just you and me.

You put a sparkle in my eyes &all these crazy butterflies, until the end of time, I'll let my heart guide these rhymes, believe me when I tell you if I had to choose, between you and the sun, I'd be nocturnal for you.

I keep telling them that I wish to be free, they can only view what I choose for them to see, you understand the feeling, not being able to breathe, and you help me escape, so I turn to my dreams.

In a world of my creation, that's where we meet,
my vision of perfection and I fall at your feet,
surely I'm the one, who should be in control,
in control of my mind, body and soul.

Then why do I continue to write, determined I will
win this fight, like I said before, with a click of your
fingers, I'm weak for you, time almost lingers.

Maybe more than lingers, each day is longer than the
last, I keep counting them down, a day further away from
our past, but a day closer to the future and all that it
could bring, maybe in the end, it doesn't matter if I win.

Winning will only fill me with pride, but that's
not what I want, believe me I've tried, I've tried
to build confidence but I still choose to hide, this
life is what I've made it, nothing but a lie.

That's why I write for you, I won't stop 'till
I hit perfection, when this book is shown, I
swear it's for your inspection, your words
inspired me, to be a better human, to love with
all my heart, to get past any confusion.

We're forever being haunted, our lingering past,
holding on to those moments, that went so fast, this
control is what I need to be freed from, I need to
find myself, and home is just not where I belong.

Every year, there's a certain time, a time
marked thoroughly in my mind, I know you
feel it too, when summer comes to town, it felt
like christmas when you were around.

I know I shouldn't but I question why, why I can barely
get through July, when I know I should be glad you're
happy, and forgetting how close you once were to me.

Even if you only had the smallest bit of faith,
it's enough for me to feel strong, I won't let it
go to waste, every day is a chance to progress,
to heal the wounds that our past left.

So every night I pray, pray you'll visit me, visit
my dreams, to help me find the key, the one I
lost long ago, the key to your heart, I should've
kept hold of it, right from the start.

I'm forever guided, pushed to explore, I know
that I'm looking, but for what, I'm not sure,
always searching, and hunting for more, maybe
my journey will bring me closer to yours.

I was dreaming again, last night we went away, we lost
ourselves in the bright lights, I wished that we could
stay, the city of Las Vegas, attracted by the colours, I'm
telling you these dreams cannot compare to the others.

Because we each have a different story, but one
thing we all think the same, we don't wish upon
anyone else to go through our mistakes, I urge to the
readers, you can't run from your problems, no matter
what happens, that's not going to solve them.

You have to stand up, no matter what they say, find a
way to get through, you'll be proud of yourself someday,
once you've come out the other end feeling so brave,
you'll be thankful to what gave you faith every day.

Her words pulled me through, but I need to do
this on my own, if I'm honest, the only thing that
helps is being alone, so every night I hope and pray,
that some day soon, I'll find a different way.

Deep down I fear you will forget me, I don't ask
for forgiveness just for you to read, remember
who I am the way that I glare, my style, the way
I do my hair, my words, gestures, the things I
wear, that look I gave you mistook for a stare.

If only you knew, no one else can compare, it's taken
too long but now I'm aware, while I've been away,
every night I prepare, prepare to leave myself open to
despair, because those feelings you had are no longer
there, they faded before my words I could declare.

When I've been selfish, your heart you still give,
so you can have mine, for aslong as I live, I trust
you, and trust your intentions are good, never
given me doubt, I knew you never would.

Even when I did wrong, you stood by my side,
that's why I'm telling them, no word I've written
is a lie, I fall at your feet, I don't care about pride,
for us I'll stand up, never again will I hide.

When you're with me, I am most at ease, we embrace
and I hold you with delicacy, my words, sounds familar,
I've said them a thousand times before, but they
don't mean a thing, my actions mean a lot more.

This journey that I travel leads me to you, this
won't be the last time even if I had to choose,
it's tiring and long, but so worth the wait, when
you're next to me, I feel guided by fate.

You make me the happiest just with your smile,
put your hand in mine and I'll stay for a while,
I can't wait to see you, I wish to be there, your
vibrant blue eyes, make me believe you still care.

I'm sitting here wasted, creating these rhymes, I
should be with you having the time of our lives,
there are just two options, be either bound or
free, a big decision, which for me seems easy.

If I could step out of my shoes, and be led another
way, I'll always look back, &wish I had stayed, you're
my world, there's nowhere else I'd rather be, to
me you are perfect, why would I want to leave.

When I see you again, it will be too soon, to declare
this love I've always had for you, you had a taste, before
I left, but before I go, you need to know the rest.

When I'm beside you, looking in your eyes, I'm thankful
for every moment, and thank God I'm alive, I can't show
you how I feel, when you're not here with me, but I cannot
ask for more when you are, it's less real than a dream.

The thoughts of our past haunt me, they're as
frequent as I breathe, we're miles apart, but you can
have my heart, because you're all I'll ever need.

As I have sinned, I'll be sent underground, but until
they day I fall, to you I am bound, some moments
are just for us, they cannot be repeated, all we
have is memories, that cannot be deleted.

Another chance has come for me to hold your
hand, this time I won't let go and nothing comes
between our plans, no surprises, nothing in our
way, I wont leave you this time, I promise to stay.

I know that you want this but need to be sure, I can
tell you there's only one thing the same as before,
my heart is in love with you I cannot ignore, I give
you my word, that each day I love you more.

When you hold my hand I forget that we, have a life
beyond just you and me, I forget my words, forget to
breathe, &this hold you have, everyone can see.

A portrait of you could be a work of art, if it
captured your flaws &the storm in your heart,
I slowly lose my mind with every breath,
thinking of the promises I should've kept.

As my mind wonders, with thoughts of you, I think of all
I promised we'd do, just like a fairytale, we wished to be
free, but my lies tore through and I broke you and me.

I know I've got my problems, I don't come free, but
you see something that I can't see, something that
you've found in me, you give me faith in my destiny.

When the heat of the summer made drowsy the
land, you sat with me contently and held my hand,
there is danger where I move my feet, lightning
flies as and when I speak, I'm oblivious to everyone
there, the danger is gone, you cleared the air.

Under snow heavy clouds there's a silent breeze, powers
like yours make me fall to my knees, I look up at you with
hope in my eyes, in your hands is where my future lies.

In the early hours of the morning that few are awake to
see, I can hear the birds chatter, how lucky they are to be
free, with no cares in the world, stretching their wings by
flight, it's true when they say nature's most alive at night.

What people would give to be a bird in the sky,
what could be better than no reasons to cry, no
worries about the time that goes by, that's how
I feel, you take my hand and take me high.

If this was a game with the prize being you, I would
never give up, no matter what I'd been through,
because it isn't just me, that's had a hard time, I
put them before you and invented each lie.

So I'll treat this like a game, a fight 'till the death, I'll
stand with no army, you can take my last breath, for
my moment of glory, I'll find a way, to carry on, this
time I wish to stay, allow me to prevail, so I can hear
that voice, I'd be there right now, if I had the choice.

I woke up lost again, I missed you last night,
it's like I need a map, everytime I lose your
light, I will concider you, in every decision,
you healed my mind, and every incision.

I know how much I mean to you, when you say
you listened to our song, I'm sure it was easy
to remember all that I've done wrong.

You let your guard down, I took advantage of your
love, it's not true when they say the decision is made
above, the power is in your hands, I'm giving it to
you now, I love you &to you I'm forever bound.

When I breathe, it's to the rhythm of your heart, I
am changed by this alchemy, so why are we apart,
I feel drawn to you, I'm being pulled by something,
this love we have binds us tighter than a ring.

When you're away the world couldn't be duller, but
when I see you it fills with colour, in our hearts this love
eternally lies, we see it in the deepness of our eyes.

I don't know what I've said to make you understand,
but I love when you smile as you reach for my
hand, what have I said, I can never tell, when
I say that I love you, you say it as well.

Though I'm not speaking there's an endless list,
reasons that I love you and why without you I can't
exist, I hope you believe every word that I've said,
because your heart's where I lay my head.

When I say that you're perfect, what I mean is you're
perfect for me, I don't want to be anywhere but with
you, even when you're angry, I know no one's right
all the time, but I'll stand beside you if you're wrong,
what you call your imperfections, I've loved all along.

If you were the moon &I were the sun, you'd
know that for me you're the only one, I would
die every night so that you could breathe, and
promise I'll come back each time that I leave.

I've said that you inspire me but I can't explain
how, nothing makes me feel better than when
you're around, I know this is something we can get
through, you need to know that I'm missing you.

I miss your voice and the way you say my name,
this distance has caused us so much pain, it
feels like a challenge to make us strong enough
to last, &not let us be defined by our past.

As we've grown apart we're different people now,
you've changed so much and I want to see how,
I've changed too and I know you can see, but can
you feel that my heart still wants you and me.

Don't need a genie a bottle, all I want is you, don't
need the room to breathe, I haven't been able to,
since the day I left I thought I could carry on, my
heart slowly tore everytime I heard our song.

But I can feel myself strengthen each time that I
write, much like a feather I am to be light, with
nothing against me or holding me down, like
this guilt I seem to be carrying around.

I'll make up for all the things that I did, I'm
thankful for each &every day that I live, because
I know that someone draws a smile on your face,
and I'll love another but I won't replace.

I'll never be too far away, and I promise every
word I've scribbled is true, there will always be a
place, in my heart reserved for you, we've said it
before, this world could leave us anyday, because
our love is undying, it will never fade away.

Another night, my memories live on, imagine me
without you, every page would be gone, what I'd
give to hear you, say my name once more, I'd fight
my way through hell, earth's center, the core.

A puppet being guided, I feel it in my veins, fate draws
me to you, whenever you call my name, sometimes I
wonder myself, why this took so long to write, but it
shows my dedication, worth every sleepless night.

I know there are only good reasons, why I'm
writing this book, but maybe I wish that one
day, I'll be unhooked, free from this hold,
you've always had on me, but I know that
i'll still see you, everytime I fall asleep.

I used to be the strength that raised you up high,
now I'm the one with my head in the skies, here
I stand alone with you in my heart, in my head
I keep looking back, right back to the start.

Be thankful for the nights that turned into mornings, friends that turned into family, &dreams that turned into reality

~ V ~

LEAVING YOU BEHIND/MOVING ON

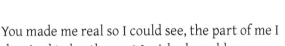

You made me real so I could see, the part of me I
despised to be, the part I wished would go away,
and make me real enough, so that you'd stay.

I'll always remember, the empty look on your face, I
couldn't be what you wanted, I put those years to waste,
all those messed up chances, apologies, and glances,
they're all on replay, and in my mind they will stay.

I've had too many chances, and wasted each one, if
I could fix my mistakes, we wouldn't have to move
on, I'm going to stay honest, to benefit ourselves, my
feet have been hurting, from all these eggshells.

I know things have changed, but some things stay a
while, I still know how to make you laugh, what I'd give
to see your smile, &i thought if I could show you these
words, things would fall back into place, I hope and
pray but I know, these past few years I can't replace.

The second I left your side, I knew it was wrong, thought
I could come back, but I'd left it for too long, because
we didn't talk, you thought I'd moved on, the silly thing
is that I still love you, &with you I'll always belong.

My instinct made me leave, I guess for a little time to
breathe, we can agree it's done us both some good,
It's brought us closer, we knew deep down it would,
you finally heard what's been on my mind, if months
and years are what you want, I'll give you the time.

You can have all the time you need, to let this sink
in, but be open to my words, I gave them everything,
every second of my time, just for them to show, that
what I did was wrong, &that time has really flown.

We stood by to watch each other grow, it's nearly
been ten years since I met you, you know, when I
look back, it doesn't feel like a long time, I remember
losing myself somewhere down the line.

Dont think, it just complicates things.
Just feel, and if it feels like home, follow its path
R.M.Drake

~ VI ~

DREAMS

Most of us have had a nightmare, I'm grateful mine
aren't that bad, one night I swear nothing can
compare, to the dream of you I had, you taking my
hand, I could ask for nothing more, the happiest
you've seen me, is a smile you never saw.

I thought trusting my head over my heart was
the right thing to do, writing endlessly &sitting
here without you, I know on the other side of
heartbreak is wisdom, but when these memories
stop haunting me, I know I'll miss them.

You've been the girl in my dreams with flowers in
your hair, but the demons in your head made your
world dark with despair, I tried to rearrange the
madness in your mind, so you could take the love
in your soul, &leave everything else behind.

I've said that you're the colour, 'your vibrant blue
eyes', painting over all of my deep red lies, now our
memories are black, darker than they seem, but I look
back into your eyes &fall deeper than a dream.

You are behind my every good deed, always bring out
the best in me, no more nightmares, you overpower
my dreams, the only place, where we can be free.

Something I wish that you could see, all those perfect
words you can believe, my promises are kept, you know
I'll never leave, so stay here and smile with ease.

I know I won't fade, when you're here with me,
it just feels right, what they call destiny, just
give me the strength, on your powers I feed, you
make me superhuman, in my hour of need.

As I dreamt of slipping into your arms, I
dropped so low at your every command, your
skills corrupted me, I'd never been lured, you
did it unknowingly, it was the only cure.

Countless times, the sound of your voice
stopped me falling apart, after everything,
you're the only one who owns my heart.

What I dreamt of was a paradise, with rain as cold as
ice, but the rays of the sun warmed our skin, as we
stepped into the sea, for one last swim, I search for her
footprints they pave the way for me to follow, &I know
I won't give up because I can't predict tomorrow.

When I was young, I failed to stay, &I thought
I'd have nothing left to say, they tell us life is for
living, I don't want to be just a memory, forever
run away with me, every night for all eternity.

All these words I write, can't explain how I feel, my
subtle dreams are all that seem real, a sanctuary,
an escape, from everything that feels fake,
material things, the air I breathe you can take.

You were sent from above to create this place,
somewhere to breathe a world I can face, these
crazy dreams are a sanctuary for me, this
used to be as easy as it was to breathe.

You are the answer to all of my prayers, I don't
wish to sleep unless you meet me there, like
I said before, I don't ask to be forgiven, I just
wish for you, to read the pages I've written.

This love feels like a water like essence, everytime
I feel you I drown in your presence, I know
this is me and just my crazy dream, but with
you is the best place that I've ever been.

I have the urge to close my eyes but I've only just
begun, I'm reminded of progression with each rise of
the sun, every day is new &full of mystery, though
for now I must dream, dream of what could be.

Another night is dawning, the dreams leave
me numb, why would I wish for morning,
when there's a chance that you will come.

I'm not asking for much, not even a reply, just for
you to know, for you to see that we can fly, if you
take my hand, I'll take us high, &you can watch
while our names, are written in the sky.

~ J. SuperMad ~

I want you to dream that I'm yours and I'll dream
that you're mine, I dream of our future, way
down the line, looking back on all the precious
times, every memory that I can find.

Another day I look at our picture, I keep it
by my beside so that I don't miss her, in an
empty place I can hear her whisper, telling me
that things can never be how they were.

I hear my name flowing with her breath, I'll try to find
her but there's not much time left, at any moment I'll
start to realise, realise before I can meet with her eyes.

Calling out for her, I wish that I could, but it would go
unheard so here I'm stood, in the middle of nowhere with
a soft echo, leading me to a place that I've never known.

Once again you appear &I fall at your feet, it's music
to my ears as I hear you speak, I wonder what could of
been, if only you knew, this love is from deep within.

Tonight I hope my dreams bring you here,
most of them remain unclear, I feel better in
every way when I have you near, keep me safe
at night, when my dreams are full of fear.

Soon as we walked in, that's when it started, all eyes on
us, because they thought we'd parted, but I walked along,
with you by my side, you held my hand, filling me with
pride, because this is the place, where there no need
to hide, and we're finally showing how we feel inside.

It drives me crazy when you say my name, I know
I only have myself to blame, but say it softly,
so only I can hear, I'll pull you nearer, closer to
my ear, invite me in to taste it on your lips, I'd
be lying if I told you this was passionless.

You don't know this but in my world, you play
the biggest part, brighten the skies, the smile
on my face, bring sweet solace to my heart.

I might not be everything that you need, but my soul
is yours I wish you could see, I notice that when I'm
with you, my head is in the skies, but in my words
and in my heart, is where true devotion lies.

There will never be a last time, that I'll hear you say my
name, you're carved into my memory, every dream is
near enough the same, through the nights I lay confused,
wonder how I get back to you, how to keep control
when I'm not awake, another night that I cannot take.

You're wrapped around my thoughts, I never wish to
wake, sanctuary for us, this is what we can create, a
step closer everyday, feels like a lifetime I've waited,
to find this place, I never thought could be created.

Another night I wish for you, to visit my dreams the way
that you do, every night without fail, you find me there
&I follow your trail, I watch as you lead me to, a place for
only me and you, until I wake and my dreams fade away, I
wish for the night to come, and this time for you to stay.

As I see you there, in a world without hate, my vision
of perfection, why would I want to escape, I kiss you
on your forehead to let you know of my devotion,
every moment we share is a force of emotion.

Would you keep me forever, something I never
though could be, if it's only there I can see you,
escape into my dreams with me, I know that these
dreams are nothing but an illusion, but you're the
one who breaks through all my confusion.

You are my air, these dreams keep me alive, because
the way I see it, if I'm dreaming I can't die, what I'm
trying to say, is I have purpose to survive, to write
the words you're reading, they are my disguise.

So visit me again tonight, while I'm fast asleep, take
me somewhere colourful, where the hills are steep,
where we can walk for miles, let me listen to you speak,
words so soft, words that make me feel complete.

Somewhere we can lay, somewhere undisturbed,
where your laughs of happiness, are the only
sounds heard, these uncontrollable dreams, are
what keep me believing, that I may have another
chance, for as long as I'm still breathing.

Feels like I'm losing sight, I've searched but can't
find, all I know is my dreams are unoccupied,
once again I'm falling asleep, wondering if you
dream of me, I dream of the promises I couldn't
keep, the ground collapsing beneath my feet.

Wishing I could remember, when I'm fast asleep,
remember the words you say, everytime you speak,
because they're more than words, they affect the way I
feel, but by then I realise, none of this can even be real.

Another escape, as I see you there I pray not to wake, it
has to be impossible for me to make the same mistake,
that's why I ask now, my hand is for you to take.

I don't have to ask why, this is just how it's meant
to be, no one else can compare, to the girl of my
dreams, when you walk my way, my heart picks up
speed, just like an addiction, not a want it's a need.

I haven't dreamt of you in a while, the only
way I can see your smile, so last night meant
more to me, than it would normally.

Walking out into the fresh air, I never expected you
to be there, the rays of the sun were all I could see,
my vision cleared, &you were waiting there for me.

With that look on your face, you waited so patiently,
while each step I took, you looked into my eyes
contently, like you would wait for all of eternity,
because you know that's how I like to dream.

I can hear the clock ticking it feels like a reminder, every
dream is on a timer &I'm forever trying to find her, when
I wake in the morning, anxious I know I'll feel, hoping
you'll be there, to wrap your arms around me for real.

I'll stall for a few seconds, to take it all in, I
know that you're not just a prize I can win, but
I've struck gold in the form of your love, and I'm
thankful that you, are the one I dream of.

Believe in your dreams,
they were given to you for a reason

I'm curious about, what will inspire me next,
the summer's on it's way, I would say it's crept,
time has gone so fast, but I've been preparing, for
what there is to come, no matter how daring.

I keep talking about how I wish to be free, my writing
always turns to my dreams, lately I've been saying I don't
wish to talk, things would be easier, if only I could walk.

Or even be like a bird, no more wishing to be
freed, being with you is really all I need, like I
said before, they can't see what's inside, they
can't see the secrets, and things that I hide.

Things I can never let them all see, it's one of my fears,
but for you I'll set it free, because I have nothing but my
honesty, I owe it to you, for every chance you've given me.

Once again I'm writing away, each time is always
longer than a page, I hoped to keep it short &as simple
as I can, I guess I could say that didn't go to plan.

I'm confessing all my fears, everything
you've never heard, I try to keep my
sanity, but I lose it with every word.

One step closer, the future is my motivation, my
goal is this, my creation, I couldn't ask for more, or
better inspiration, I write for one, my dedication.

I write these words because it's the only way I know
how, I thought that this would be a good way to show I'm
bound, you know we can be better than how we were,
I'm planning you will read this, as an intimate whisper.

My soul lays buried in the ink that writes, I unveil
my thoughts every single night, seems this is how it's
always been, this love breathes life into my dreams.

So many words, though I don't know what to
write, the thunder has kept me up through most
of the night, inspiration, here and there, my love
for you is easy, like the way I breathe air.

I'll try to write about, anything new, but
every sentence I start, ends with you.

I apoligise for being wrong, letting you feel lonely,
I should've been there, and you can blame me,
I have been punished, for the mess I'd made,
you can see the marks that karma gave.

But here I stand strong, I used to be afraid, now I realise,
this debt must be paid, so this is what I'll do, every night
and every day, my last wish is that you read every page.

If this was the way back into your heart, the
journey would be like a crumbling path, I'm
still inspired even though we're apart, &I'm
drawn by the distant echo of your laugh.

I say you leave me breathless, because my words
comes out wrong, so I write them on paper,
seems that's where they belong, I write so much
about me, you and confusion, it sounds silly
but I'm just inspired by every illusion.

Every dream my mind creates, I try to chase it before
it escapes, and I'm just left with nothing but reality, be
honest, that's where no one wants to be, but with you,
it seems like I've missed every chance, I just want to
make a home, make you feel beautiful, make you laugh.

I've been writing for a long time, I cannot help creating
a rhyme, it feels as though it's a crime, if I don't write
down every line, every word that appears in my
mind, this love I have for you, I attempt to define.

The only sense of freedom I feel, is writing this book, it
makes this seem real, like everything will work out in
the end, this will be the longest letter that I'll ever send.

The lyrics to our song, always kept us strong, even when
things went wrong, you knew I'd love you all along, I
want my words to take you away, so you can see, I write
this for you and hope that one day, you'll trust me.

I write these words, without hesitation, each
line calms, every frustration, I don't count
myself as lucky, it's more like I'm blessed, to find
someone like you, some people never rest.

You're the reason that these words are written,
it would be an understatement to say that I'm
smitten, every sentence is because you inspire,
with every touch my heart is on fire.

I'm devoted to you it goes without saying, but
maybe you're not the only one who needs saving.

In all honesty, I've been awake all night, staring
at these pages, I just want to write, write about
your smile, because it gets me everytime, these
are your powers, they inspire me to rhyme.

I've been thinking about you, from my mind
you're never leaving, soon as I wake to when I
fall asleep, you're the only one I'm needing.

I keep feeling that I've written all I can, it's like
I'm slowly giving up but that wasn't the plan, I
plan to keep writing for as long as I breathe, it
keeps me on track, it's what I do in-between.

When I haven't got you here by my side, I regret each
and every time that I lied, I know you're waiting to take
the next step, to see if I'm true &my promises are kept.

My pages are written, I say they're to prove, prove
my devotion, I write all this for you, to show
every moment that we share is true, that there's
nothing in this world that I wouldn't do.

To get me in the zone I sit by candle light, reach
for my old pen &I start to write, about the
things we don't say anymore, deep in the heart,
the center, the core, sometimes I struggle to
describe this feeling, but I have faith that you'll
be there when I'm far away and dreaming.

Believe me when I say I'm not here to waste your
time, I know that your hand still fits perfectly
with mine, I've said time is wasted when I'm not
with you, so writing is all that I seem to do.

They tell me I get writers block, but I never thought
these words would stop, even though it's hard,
sometimes these words flow like rain, because
you still inspire me, &that will never change.

The worst thing is when I can't find the words to
write, I know what I want to say but that's only half
the fight, the other half is to get each word correct, so
you don't think of this as anything less than perfect.

You're the only one I want near when I'm down, I still
feel you close to me even though you're not around,
but I don't quite understand why I think we're meant
to be, I guess it's because I still see you in my dreams.

I look at every blank page as a chance to prove,
prove that I can stick by, be devoted and true,
these pages I write are much more than words,
they give you power, everything you deserve.

I describe your powers as a cruel curse, only because
I can't imagine what's worse, I could leave everything
behind &start somewhere new, but none of it
would work because I know I'm devoted to you.

And I know you'll always hold this power, that
makes my heart race a hundred miles an hour, I've
been trying to plan the words I need to say, but
when I'm with you all of my thoughts fly away.

I always thought of my writing as creative, a gift,
but something's changed, &I cannot resist, as
much as I wish to stop, these words still flow, it
feels like the work of the man down below.

It's as though someone's given me the gift of
rhymes, but with it comes the curse of all time,
as I keep writing I can't extinguish, this fire
that burns, it will burn 'till I'm finished.

The reason I'm telling you it's a curse, like I
said, I can't imagine what's worse, if writing
this much, doesn't bring you back to me, I guess
I'll have to find another way to be free.

I hope atleast once that you've wished me near, we
planned our future but ended up here, I know I
caused this &I promise take the blame, my words
are here to assure you that I'd never do the same.

I don't believe them when they say that I'm gifted,
because there's nothing but lines when my pen is
lifted, really I'm just lost, lost in every thought, focused
on my dreams, to reflect what I've been taught.

When we're apart I write these words all day, but I don't
say half of what I wish to say, when you're standing
there with nothing in my way, I lose my words and
quickly I pray, I pray that I've given you the powers
to see, see that you've made me the best I can be.

I've been thinking about you all night, the inspiration
is there so I'm able to write, just seems like this is my
endless fight, to carry on I must be one brave knight.

I don't have to look down because I know
where I stand, I ask for you to let me, &with no
hesitation I'll take your hand, I'm brave enough
now, I say it like I'm walking beyond the line, I
wish to fight for us, our love is not a crime.

If it wasn't for you I wouldn't be writing, I wouldn't
be winning this battle I'm fighting, you wanted
me to move on, I know I should be trying, if I
ever say I have, I hope you know I'm lying.

I want to be able to say that I've tried, I know I can't
take back each time I've lied, at times I feel ready, then
something tells me I'm not, as I continue to write, I find it
harder to stop, when I reach the end and you see that I'm
done, you'll know that I'll love you for every year to come.

There are times when I think I shouldn't be writing,
but I have some faith and it keeps me fighting, I
want to show you that I've learnt from my mistakes,
if you walk with me, I promise you'll be safe.

I know that you'll question, why these words are
so late, but this needed to be perfect so I tampered
with fate, I look up at the stars, they brighten my
night, these pages are full, yet I continue to write.

Sometimes I imagine how our future would
be, with nothing between us, just you and me,
the feeling you give me makes me feel brave,
like I'm the only one that you'll ever save.

When it takes over, it leaves me feeling numb, without
it I'm nothing but what I've become, this is why I write,
because even when I'm not there it's true, I think how
can I explain something that's as amazing as you.

The moon is awake and I'm prepared to write,
about this mourningful, cold, rainy night, the
street lights are on but there's no one around,
no one to hear all the distant sounds.

Through the glass windows I know you can see,
the people enthralled by this book as they read, I
sense that each of you are on the same page, as you
envision the letters that resemble her name.

I'll tell you when we were young I would sin,
each lie tore through every layer of skin, I show
you these words so you know what I am, God
himself says from heaven I'm banned.

I attempted to compete with the man in the
sky, he says it's a sin to have this much pride,
filled with rage I swore my revenge, I'd been
self destructive but it wasn't the end.

I had stolen innocent hearts one after the
other, twisted them then left them to recover,
it was never enough as I indulged each one,
oblivious to the person that I'd become.

I've told you before I don't ask for forgiveness, I
just want to be good &for you to witness, that as
long as you love me I'll always be a winner, even
though my past says that I'm a deadly sinner.

I don't wish to sleep before completing a page, a page
of recovery from my sinful ways, it's hard to imagine
you being by my side, reading my words with love
in your eyes, something that's so hard to believe, I
hope that from my memory you'll never leave.

All of these years, I've wished them to fly so fast, so
that I can complete my task, each word I write defeats
the past, tonight I wish these words are my last.

Wishing that time would fly, is not positive
and definately not advised, when I'm not with
you I'm without a friend, &every time I pick
up my pen, I start to write all over again.

That's why I say this love is endless, until I'm
with you my heart just can't rest, but because
I love you, I'd do anything, when you're
ready I'll be there, patiently waiting.

When things stand in our way, and you find
me hard to believe, know that my love is pure,
&there's nowhere else I'd rather be.

Part of me doubts that things will get better, the
other half thinks it's best, to write this endless letter,
I write this to show you, that I know who I am, the
part of me that hurt you, God says is banned.

So keep these pages I need them to prove, prove I
existed only to love you, I'd rather it be you clouding my
mind, someone else would be wasting precious time.

We were just kids in love
feels like all our cherished memories were a fairytale
LOSING THE WILL TO WRITE
InspireMe ?

You miss 100% of the shots you dont take

~ VIII ~

WISHES VS FEARS

I look up at the stars whenever I feel weak, they
remind me of the strength that grew everytime
I'd hear you speak, at the top of the Eiffel tower,
that's where I'll meet you, I would climb up
that high, just to see your point of view.

I don't know whether or not, if I should keep this secret
at bay, or to surprise someone, whose name I'll never
say, I feel like these words are just not enough, to tell you
our hearts beat the same, I'd love translate this into the
language of love, but I know it will be better this way.

I'll tell them every wish because I pray so hard, I wish
for your happiness, to heal each scar, for each bad
memory to burn, so every night I can learn, learn
to set you free, and hope you'll come back to me.

I'm thankful every day, I thank the skies above,
you're God's best creation, everything I dream of,
but I'll always fear time until I feel strong, you give
me the strength to keep all these fears gone.

If I said I wasn't scared, now that would be a lie, I'm
scared that I won't get the chance to say goodbye,
I fear you wont reminisce, not a tear in your eye,
that every word I told you, you believe is a lie.

Take a moment step back and breathe, a moment to
listen, listen to me, when you look at me I believe,
looking in your eyes, you're all that I need, &even
when I leave you will never lose my love, it will be
with you forever because nothing changes up above.

I wish to be your first and last thought, I want to
free you when you get caught, the only one you'll
need to kiss, the only one you'll truly miss, I'm
hoping that you never forget about me, because
every night that I write, I want you to read.

I wish that you were by my side, if you could forgive
each time that I lied, if I ever see a time, that you wish
to stay, I would thank the Lord and have no need to
pray, because you'll lay beside me, counting the stars,
and I'll listen to the beating, of our two hearts.

As the sun sets, I can't help but wish you near,
your hand in mine can defeat every fear, my
biggest fear is why I'm writing this now, I want
this to show that to you I am bound.

The fear is, that I'm losing time, time is wasted
when you're not on my mind, I hang onto
every good memory I can find, I fear this book
will be unfinished, &be left behind.

My other fear, my mind and heart are at war,
these words don't flow as easy anymore, my
heart knows, that the ties we have are uncut,
but my brain is telling me, I should give up.

But I need to let you know, my last thought will be you, if
there's distance between us, then writing's what I'll do.

What I write is my priority, before things get worse,
before I leave, I need you to read this, so that you know
why, that my fate was this, &I'll be up in the sky.

In a perfect world, I'd be your shoulder to borrow,
I'll keep you safe in my arms, the promise of
tomorrow, I wish it was me, that could keep you
strong, be your Heroine, that helps you carry on.

I want it to be us, I want to give you a home, to take
off your shoes, &place you on your throne, you
listen patiently as I recite my last ode, knowing
you're the only one, I ever wish to show.

But I write for the readers, because they need to
know, no matter how close you are to your other half,
let them go, as one of life's challenges, one of two
things will happen, you'll find them with someone
else, or your wildest dreams, you can have them.

That's when you'll know, that you're truly meant
to be, and the rest will surely flow so easy, this is
my proposal, I want you with me, so if you ever
change your mind, you know where I'll be.

I'm stumbling as I walk, but for you I'll never
rest, anything you wish, I'll be at your request,
don't be afraid, never will you need to grieve,
because we can be together, forever you & me.

I have to be careful, it's my heart that you're holding,
I try to play my cards right, you know I'm not folding,
I've walked away before, been to different places,
but home is with you, I've got a hand full of aces.

I know I wasted those few years, and I only wish
for more, to be with you again, all the pain I
would endure, I've written this once, &I meant it
before, this love I have for you, I can't ignore.

I tried to get this perfect, every day and every night, but
I don't know whether the timing is wrong or right, if I
should wait until maybe one day you'll come back to me,
or tell you now, while we still have a chance to be free.

Read my words just in time, know that it's my heart you
teach, before you cross the line, when you're no longer
in my reach, I'll lose my inspiration when I lose your
light, my memories alone can't keep me safe at night.

I keep hoping my words are not too delayed, &wishing
it was my name, you call when you're afraid, I know
you've been waiting, for me to be strong, I'll be waiting
on my white horse, for the chance to come along.

These dreams may still haunt me, I can't escape, you're
my desire, I don't want to wait, because every second,
I swear is a waste, not being there, to see your face.

I want to give you everything, a happy life &home,
someone to lean on, somewhere to go, to be your
best friend, so you wont be alone, you're the
queen in my castle, you belong on the throne.

Another day is nearly done, I pray tonight that
maybe you'll come, I look around but you're not in
sight, maybe I'm no longer your shining light.

There is a chance that someone has taken my
place, I'll be jealous if they get to wake up to your
face, their feelings may be true, and you may feel
the same way too, but would they write endlessly
for you, they'll never have the love I do.

I know that you've moved on, or atleast that's how
it seems, but tell you'll meet me even if it's only in
your dreams, I talk about dreams, they create this
illusion, that our love would defeat all this confusion.

I'm feeling like a walking contradiction, what I'm writing
is part truth, and partly fiction, the truth is I want to
be there, but a new story has begun, I can't promise
no storms, let me hold your hand through each one.

The fiction part is made up of each desire, what I'm
feeling inside &what sets my soul on fire, I know my
dreams are bigger than any fear, I keep thinking
maybe it's a good thing that you're not here.

This is what you want for us, for me to be your friend,
maybe the beauty of the world, will inspire me again,
I just hope this way, our voices are heard, &that my
actions mean so much more than each &every word.

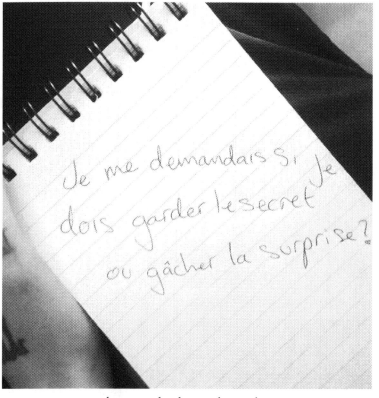

Debating whether to keep this a
secret, or spoil the surprise

Redamancy;
The act of loving the one who loves you,
a love returned in full

~ IX ~

HER TURN

Now that you've seen, what I present to them,
the rest is for you, right down to the end, you're
the only secret I can't keep, they need to know,
you're my last thought when I sleep.

I know I will regret this if I don't try, &I won't
stand a chance to show I won't lie, a chance to
be myself, to tell them all the truth, that this
was meant to be, &that I was made for you.

After all this time, I still get butterflies, I try to
hide it, but this I can't disguise, you do something
to me, I'm under your spell, I'm powerless
around you, but I know you can't tell.

Because I tell you, I'd fight 'till the end, it is the truth, I
will not pretend, but I'd do so much more, because you
deserve, deserve my honesty, to be the only one I serve.

You asked me to be patient, I'm not the one in
control, you don't realise you own, my mind, body
&soul, because I owe to you, a lifetime of love,
you deserve to be taken, to the skies &above.

These words right here, I dedicate to you, to forgive the
pain, and all I put you through, these scars remind us,
they won't go away, they were jaded, carved, the debt
I must repay, a lifetime of debt, that I owe to you, now
you're not the only one, who knows what it's due to.

I'm sure after what I put you through, you could break
my heart and I'd still forgive you, are you ready to make
a choice, the decision is all yours, the power is in your
hands now, remember that when it rains it pours.

When your hands hold, the gift that I give,
there's no turning back, destroy this or let
live, there are the only ways it can go, I fear
your shoulder will be as cold as snow.

I can bet they're all thinking, why not write about
something new, but this is your time to shine,
&every word will be true, let them know the story
from the start until this day, how I treated you
was undeniable, the lifetime debt I must repay.

But there is just, one thing that I wish, please
keep me strong, &keep faith in me through this,
you're the one who changed me and everything
I do, I do simply because I love you.

Me and you are like a deck of cards, I'll be spades
and you can be hearts, someone I can never replace,
we suit, I close my eyes, and see only your face.

I don't blame you, for the lack of affection, deep down
you may think, I'll walk in the other direction, so you
can't let your guard down, let me into your heart,
because when I left you, your faith in me fell apart.

The power is in your hands, it's coarsing through you
now, I can't help but love you, I swear to you I'm bound,
these bad memories are in the past, that's where
I will leave them, the future's bright so close your
eyes and see me, you know we dream for a reason.

In every blank space, I'll be writing your name, I
wish to be with you, every night and every day,
if you say no, I swear to not question why, you'll
find me in a place, where happiness goes to fly.

And if ever you find, someone that you love more, I'd
be happy to see you love them, it's what your heart is
for, no matter how I long, for you to be mine, I would
rather see you smile, meet me in another lifetime.

If you don't feel the same, I'm telling you there will be
no blame, I'll still love you and think that you're vain,
you're beautiful, and deserved to be known by name.

But I feel deep down, that would just make things
worse, I'd rather be subtle with every verse, I'm
very conscious of what I'm writing, because I don't
want to waste all this time I've been fighting.

When you read this, I want it to be patiently, let each
word slowly sink in as you breathe, don't focus too much
or too little, paint it in your mind, &observe the detail.

I feel it when I'm close to you, so lost in your eyes I
can't find my way through, I feel like I can touch the
sky, because you have powers that take me high.

With you I'm content, like the perks of meditation,
each line calms almost every frustration, not
being able to hold you, the way that I miss, I
feel your powers, everytime that we kiss.

Magic is often things like, card tricks and short
levitation, but I know what I feel is deeper, it has no
limitation, we don't need a crowd or a demonstration,
powers like yours, are used without hesitation.

I know that you wish I would shut this door, I just want
to show you, you're worth fighting for, I know things
have changed &they're different than before, but can you
find the words to tell me you don't love me anymore?

The future is unexpected, unplanned experiences,
hoops to jump through and fences after fences, we can't
predict the obstacles but I can promise you this, even
when I'm at my highest, you're the only one I miss.

Don't be too quick to deny how good we could be, I'd
give anything for the chance to make you feel happy,
I know that we're apart and that's how it stays for
now, if you need me just know that I'll be around.

You ignite my creativity and it's something I wish
to show, maybe this time you'll see, the more you
read the more you know, you need to know every
thought that has ever crossed my mind, like I'm
proud you've been strong since I left you behind.

Sometimes I wish you never saw the person I used
to be, &I just wish I didn't take your every word so
personally, my apologies I know will never be enough,
but everytime you fell down you always got back up.

You've always been strong and somehow always there
for me, even when things got bad you were as fierce
as could be, there were times you were crazy but I
wouldn't have it any other way, we all have flaws &I
loved yours but I wasn't honest and it wasn't okay.

So things haven't been simple &I've been away
awhile, but your powers still let you take all you
want with a smile, even though I know things won't
be the same, &I cannot repair the memories or the
pain, all I can do is stand up and take the blame,
&swear to myself to never say your name.

There is always someone who cares
for you without your knowledge

~ X ~

THE FUTURE

Before I've been bad, I showed no emotion, in your presence, you had my heart frozen, now I write, if you ask who for, I'll say it's you, you're the one I adore.

With every kiss I pray to survive, keep me forever because I hate goodbyes, but when I leave you'll see me rise, my soul will remain very much alive.

I hope that one day you find your way back to me, even if it takes you far across the seas, seeing you again plays in my head, what I'd say or do, will you hang on to the words I've said.

I'll tell you that I have a surprise, ask you then to open your eyes, as your hands unwrap the gift you receive, you look into my eyes &I promise to never leave.

I hope to always see a path that leads to you, when I'm lost in the dark be the light that guides me through, in a way I can feel our every wish becoming true, the mirror shows the sight of me wanting you.

This is the way I promise it will always be, hold onto this maybe it will set us free, this could be endless but it will go unheard, I'd love to speak if only I could find the words.

I swear this time, I'll show you I'm brave, I'll stand my ground, nothing can get in the way, I'll be the reason that you feel saved, if you find the love hidden in each page.

I want you to take pictures, enjoy the journey ahead, and I'll be right next to you, writing the words you've read, let go of our bad memories, forget the things I said, as long as I'm with you, there's nowhere I'd rather be instead.

The most content, that I've ever felt, safe with you, in your arms I could melt, I'm serious about us, and want you to believe, that I'll be at your rescue, if there's something to defeat.

I feel the warnings, I feel every sign, my brain is telling me there isn't much time, why sit here creating a rhyme, when I can find a way to leave everything behind.

Fears make me weak, I'm at my strongest when I'm with you, I only wish to sleep, because these dreams feel so true, atleast there, I have the chance to say, all that I need to, before I go away, when I leave for a place, I'll forever stay, &in these pages, my love will remain.

This is the reason, why I had to leave, I'm only sorry that it took too long for me to see, what I did was wrong, on that we can agree, I know I need to hold back, to give you the space you need.

You're safe with me I promise, I'll be your castle wall, for you I'll be strong, never will I let you fall, if you lose faith, or no longer love me anymore, know that even as we get older, my hand wont stop holding yours.

It's 4am I should be sleeping, but recently I've not been
dreaming, I'm hoping that my heart will forget, once
I've finished writing I'll have nothing to regret.

I just want that chance for us to fly, for me to be there
to kiss you goodnight, with my arms around you, I'll
keep you safe, I'll be that person, no one can replace.

I never want you to feel like you're alone, just wish
we had time to build ourselves a home, I'll say
this one more time, before I go to sleep, I swear
this time I mean it, every promise I will keep.

I miss how your arms used to comfort me, always
around on stormy nights like these, my only regret
was the way I left you, with nothing but hope to hold
on to, I know you've found someone to share your life
with, I won't hold you back but don't share your gift.

I keep telling them I can't explain your powers, one
thought of you &I end up writing for hours, our
future is so fresh, a slate that's been cleaned, I want to
make the most of it, to show you what love means.

Believe me I know I can rewrite and erase, but my
words are true, and I'll write them on every page,
sometimes I wish to forget everything, is that
what you want me to say, I can keep these feelings
hidden, but know that they'll never fade.

You were the spark that made me see clear, I
know I hadn't been right for years, I write this
for you, if you believe in shining stars, that lead
you to someone who captures your heart.

I wish you waited a little while longer, but you
want me to be your friend, like how we were at
the start, it's not the same we can't pretend, but
because I feel this way, I'll tell you what I'll bring,
honesty to this friendship, I'll be your anything.

When I'm not with you, you're on my mind, I don't
know why, we still say that we're fine, I want to
leave the skeletons of our past behind, we can
create new memories, we have a whole lifetime.

I'll be your
forever

I'll leave the
Skeletons of our past
behind,
we can create new
memories, we have a
whole lifetime.

You're one decision away from
a totally different life

~ XI ~

THE END PART 1

You don't have to ask anymore, for me to catch
you when you fall, this is my promise, I'll be there
through it all, I heard that voice again today,
the voice that makes everything else fade.

The words you say give me hope to believe, that
there may still be a chance for you and me, you
asked if I'm sure that I want a life with you, truth
is I can't find anything I would rather do.

I know that you said, we're in lives that we'll always
belong, but this is for you, I hope it will right every
wrong, you trusted me to stay, you know I regret
leaving, you gave me everything, just by breathing.

But things have changed, and we're no longer in
contact, it's been your choice, so I can't resent
that, it just means you won't know how I feel, I
want to open up to you, &show you what's real.

You wanted me to change, &for everyone to know, what
the real story was, so now I've told them how it goes,
you loved me to the skies and back, never lost faith in
me, I was the heartless one, but nobody would believe.

These are all the words I couldn't say, so I saved them
all, just for this day, I want you to hold me like you
never could, &I'll hold you tighter, like I said I would.

I know I seem so happy and care free, but I swear
no one misses you more than me, I was afraid
to scare you, tell you I'd fallen so hard, but if
only you knew, your touch left me scarred.

These words sound crazy, I think you're meant
for me, I see it in my head, feel it when I breathe,
this love won't go away, I hope we're meant to
be, I don't wish to wait, you're all that I need.

I wish this didn't scar, it's just like a tattoo, a
symbol of our history, I'm bound only to you, people
say to treasure time because it flies, but these
years away, have been the longest of my life.

Im scared that my heart, might not have many beats
left, but I've told you before, I'll love you beyond
my last breath, nothing can stop the way I feel in
my chest, not even God can lay my soul to rest.

Things are getting harder, I just wish to hear
your voice, saying that you love me, and that
I have a choice, it was the only way to see you,
every night when I'd fall asleep, I guess my lack of
dreams will make the promise easier to keep.

I'm thinking that I won't have to pretend, if this love
eventually came to an end, who knows if that will
ever be, or if you're forever the only one I see.

I know I've said you're my one and only, but the problem
is that you feel lonely, I know I can't be with you today,
but what's meant to be will always find a way.

&if by the end, you're unsure how you feel,
read it over until it seems real, when I write the
final words, believe I'm at the end, I think back
to the beginning &write it all over again.

I know that without you, I wouldn't have made it this
far, this book would be unwritten, I would have an
untamed heart, I hope by now, you can feel my words
are true, that I'll never ask for anyone but you.

You're only out of my reach because you're so far,
the only problems I saw was that we're apart, I'd
love to be the one laying next to you, but I'm not
coming back home, not atleast 'till I have to.

Memories have been creeping up on me, following
like a ghost, I keep losing my focus, when I need
it the most, I'll borrow a few words, from all
of my favourite songs, to invent a way to ask
you, what we've been waiting on all along.

I know we can make a paradise of our own,
&I can promise that you won't be alone,
together we'd have a fairytale home, see that
underneath our skin is not only bone.

Our souls are alive, don't be scared of the unknown,
think of my writing as my way to show, just talk
to me, tell me all the things I don't know, If I
promise you'll be safe with me, can we go?

We can leave what's around us, you're all I'll ever
need, your heart gives mine a reason to beat,
I'm lying when I say that I'm made of rock, one
kiss from you could make this heart soft.

You know that what we have is forever, and if
I was to die, that I'd wish to be better, better
for you, because it's what you deserve, you'll
be my last thought, the last that I'd serve.

I write to show you, that I'm way more than
smitten, to prove I can do much more than listen,
I guess you long for the comfort, that I provide,
I'll be your best friend, there's no need to hide.

In this world we each have a need, a need to love as easy
as we breathe, things are different with you, I am bound
but so free, however in the end, we each have to leave.

I say this is love, because it's the only word I know, this
feeling I can't describe, you lift me up when I feel low,
you took a piece of my heart, &made it all your own, so
even when we were apart, you were never really alone.

I leave you these pages, to remember me by, to
answer each question, so you don't have to ask
why, I can see that you're alot happier inside, you
came out of our past, better than just alive.

I'm not saying it was a struggle to survive, I'm sure
someone was there to keep your head up high,
because you came out stronger than me in my eyes,
I guess you must've found where true wisdom lies.

I keep holding on to you, because you're my faith,
always my first thought when I wake, I know
we can have the freedom, to do as we please,
if you're not afraid of what's meant to be.

I'm sure of what I want, &know what we need,
keep your hand in mine, and tell me what you
see, I'll show you the way if you walk beside me,
no battle that's worth a fight will be easy.

Thinking of how much I hurt you, that I'll regret all my
life, I want to make it up to you, for you to be my wife,
but it's your choice, whether you wish to believe, that
I can make you smile everytime that you breathe.

Your magic blinds me, you still ignite this fire,
we're far apart, but you endlessly inspire, if
your love returns to me, my heart will fly, keep
these pages, they replace every goodbye.

Remember; the greatest failure, is not to try

~ XII ~

THE END PART 2

I'd listen to you for hours &I swear you couldn't
bore me, I feel anxious to say this is the end of our
story, I guess new beginnings flow after the edge, the
borderline that divides, my past &future like a ledge.

I ask myself if I'm sure that I'm brave, diving
off this ledge I try not to stumble or delay, as
I think of all that my future could bring, you
run through my head just before I dive in.

When I look down it resembles a waterfall, behind
me I see everything I've done, &it's lurking so tall, I
think if I take the leap I could leave it behind, discover
new things because there's just so much to find.

If I go in another direction, &alone is how I wish to
stand, don't feel like there's no space for you, I'll always
give you a hand, no matter where you are or who is by
my side, I'll be honest &true even if it stuns my pride.

The future is a clean slate &we can choose any design,
we can be anything we wish, our imagination is
devine, I swear to you, I have no reason to hide, I'm
preparing this so we don't have to say goodbye.

I'm asking you to be there, to hold my hand
through the rest, stand by my side, &be the one
who knows me best, I want you to be sure, I can't
lose your faith, not again, I'll heal your bruises
&scars, I'll be there to carry you 'till the end.

Late at night I think of you, wishing I could call,
then I think you may not want to talk at all, if
you are happy with the way things are, then
I'll leave, but you need to keep my heart.

It's bound to you, wherever I go, even when I
end up six feet below, I need you to save these
pages, save them for when I leave, so that you
know I love you, you're the reason I breathe.

That's why I feel the need to write, so that you
can see, all those words you long to hear, they
hide themselves within me, I will always be the
healer, that healed all your scars, even the ones
I gave, the ones marked on your heart.

I hated myself, to see what I had given, I was so
wrong to hurt you, I never want to be forgiven, I
only ask for you, to see what I've become, and for
you to know, that you'll always be the only one.

This is your turn to break my heart, you can take my
hand, or watch it fall apart, whatever you wish, I will
do, this book is my life, and I'm handing it to you.

You've given me all the space I need, but I still think of
you everytime that I breathe, I'm writing almost everyday
so that you can see, I'm devoted to being the best I can be.

So I promise to try, and patiently wait, I urge for you,
my secret escape, I have faith one day, that I'll be,
everything you wished, kind, brave, and family.

I know this is messed up, and I can't make it right,
but you'll always be my angel, every day and every
night, I'm not doubtful, I'll love you 'till we part,
because of you I have a pure and honest heart.

So this is our story, from all that I know, you are the only
one I ever wish to show, like I said before I write for them
too, to open their minds, to help them get through.

I know I wasn't there for you at your worst,
but every night I wasn't, believe me I cursed,
everytime I returned, I had hope in my eyes,
but now do you still believe that's a lie?

This book is my life, all I wish I could say, I have
faith it will get to you, and that's why I pray,
I pray that maybe one day you'll see, I love
you deeper, than you could ever love me.

To know that you were the one, who made an impact,
knowing you changed me for the better, I admit
that, I can't say I enjoy the way things are right
now, but in the end I hope you find me around.

As much as anyone likes to be in control, I give to you,
my mind and soul, I'm willing because I belong to
you, that's how it's meant to be, no reason to argue.

I'm reminded by the things that I find, all the memories
that we've left behind, I wonder if, out of all mankind,
if I'm on the right path, and it's you I had to find.

I lose my breath with every thought, to chase my dreams
is what I've been taught, I have ran for what seems like
so long, telling you I love you, and that we belong.

Every now and again, I get a burst of inspiration,
my writing improves with my dedication, I'm
telling you there's no better motivation, than
my love for you, it's my only salvation.

It's been another whirlwind, I haven't wrote
in so long, the lack of dreams, my sanctuary,
where nothing was ever wrong, unlike in the real
world, where I can't hold you like I wish, and I'm
not the one who feels, your goodnight kiss.

You told me there was someone else, I didn't ask
for you to wait, I knew you must've been lonely,
right now I could just escape, because I feel like a
fool, for loving you like this, when someone else
is holding you, when I'm not the one you miss.

I have to accept, that someone else has your heart,
this is what you deserve, a beautiful, fresh start,
I'm sure by now, you can decide, do you have faith
left in me, or still believe every word is a lie?

They know that I'm yours and that's how it will
stay, keep my heart, you're the only one it will
obey, my undying love for you, I'll take to my
grave, and say no more, as I aim to be brave.

Now the chase is over, you want me to move on, I never
want to let go, but I know if it's not right, it's wrong,
so I'll write one last page, but from now until the end,
I'll be here for you, in me you'll always have a friend.

I was her everything, her heart and soul, she
thought she'd dug her grave, but I pulled her
from that hole, when she was lost in the dark, I
was her shining light, she said I chased away the
darkness that haunted her dreams at night.

She said I was the strength that carried her to tomorrow,
that I was the hope, replacing her ever-lasting sorrow,
she called me her healer because I healed all her scars,
that I was her angel, sent from the brightest of stars.

I must've been the joy, that filled her empty heart,
because I made her life whole, when it was falling
apart, when she found me, she was freed from all
torment, I was her angel, that was heaven sent.

She said I meant so much to her, the only one she adored,
said I was her everything, she could ask for nothing more.

Many nights, I sit here and write,
You're the reason I stay up all night.

So you'll see me with a pad and pen,
Only writing that I love you as more than a friend.
Usually I don't hide it, I want to show you it's real,
Lies are what you asked for, that was the deal.

In time I hope that you change your mind,
So I can show you, your hand was meant for mine.

You want me in your life, but I cannot take your hand,
Obviously we need time, that I understand.
Us together in the end, is my only wish,
Relax with me in paradise, let us share a kiss.

Supermad, x